Zip It!

WRITTEN BY
Jane Lindaman

ILLUSTRATIONS BY
Nancy Carlson

XYZPDQ

CAROLRHODA BOOKS • MINNEAPOLIS

Dedicated to Spencer, Hayden, Jeff, Dean, Jeff, Rex, and Mark. —J.L.

Dedicated to elastic pant waists! —N.C.

It all started when Dad and I were leaving to run some errands one Saturday.

Text copyright © 2012 by Jane Lindaman
Illustrations copyright © 2012 by Nancy Carlson

Carolrhoda Books
A division of Lerner Publishing Group, Inc.
241 First Avenue North
Minneapolis, MN 55401 U.S.A.

Website address: www.lernerbooks.com

Main body text set in Kidprint MT Std 31/28. Typeface provided by Monotype Typography.

Library of Congress Cataloging-in-Publication Data

Lindaman, Jane.
    Zip it! / by Jane Lindaman ; illustrated by Nancy Carlson.
        p.   cm.
    Summary: Joe tries to warn his busy father about an embarrassing trouser oversight.
    ISBN: 978-0-7613-5592-2 (lib. bdg. : alk. paper)
    [1. Parent and child—Fiction. 2. Humorous stories.] I. Carlson, Nancy L., ill. II. Title.
PZ7.L6569Zi 2012
[E]—dc23   2011021240

Manufactured in the United States of America
1 - BC - 12/31/11

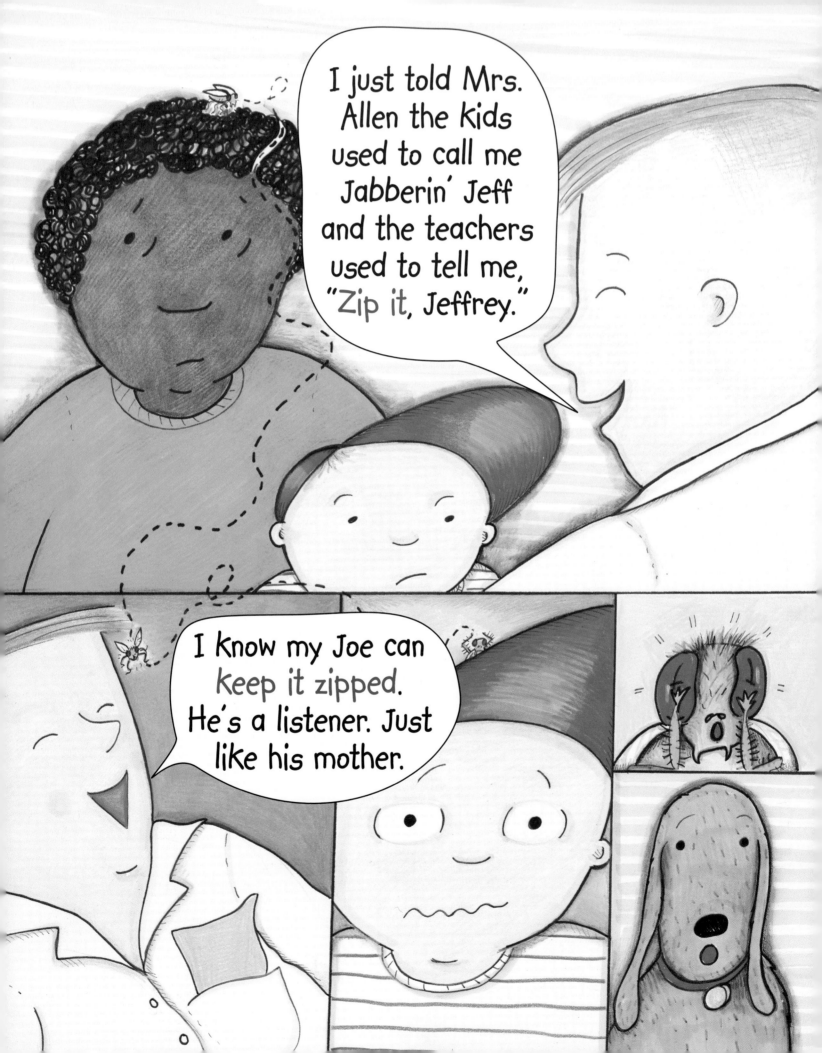